For my great-uncle Joe Manning who said,
"Go be an artist. The world needs more artists."

Copyright © 2017 by Jeff Mack.
All rights reserved. No part of this book may be reproduced in any form without written permission from the publisher.

Library of Congress Cataloging-in-Publication Data
Names: Mack, Jeff, author, illustrator.
Title: Mine! / by Jeff Mack.
Description: San Francisco, California : Chronicle Books LLC, [2017] | Summary:
Two mice argue with increasing heat over their mutual border, until someone bigger intervenes.
Identifiers: LCCN 2016013910 | ISBN 9781452152349 (alk. paper)
Subjects: LCSH: Mice—Juvenile fiction. | Animals—Juvenile fiction. | Possessiveness—Juvenile fiction. |
Quarreling—Juvenile fiction. | CYAC: Mice—Fiction. | Animals—Fiction. | Sharing—Fiction. | Quarreling—Fiction
Classification: LCC PZ7.M18973 Mi 2017 | DDC 813.6 [E] —dc23 LC record available at https://lccn.loc.gov/2016013910

Manufactured in China.

FSC
www.fsc.org
MIX
Paper from
responsible sources
FSC™ C008047

Design by Sara Gillingham Studio.
Handlettering by Jeff Mack.
The illustrations in this book were rendered in mixed media.

10 9 8 7 6 5 4 3 2 1

Chronicle Books LLC
680 Second Street
San Francisco, California 94107

Chronicle Books—we see things differently. Become part of our community at www.chroniclekids.com.

MINE!

JEFF MACK

chronicle books · san francisco